Bootsie's Big '50s

by
OLLIE HARRINGTON

About Comics
Camarillo, California

Bootsie's Big '50s

These cartoon panels originally appeared in *The Pittsburgh Courier* from 1954 through 1958. The reproductions were made using the best sources available to the publisher.

Cartoons copyright © Dr. Helma Harrington, Berlin. Used by permission.

This compilation copyright 2021 About Comics.

Continuous printing beginning January, 2022

ISBN (paperback): 978-1-949996-35-7

For bulk purchases, wholesale orders, customized editions, and other inquiries, email *questions@aboutcomics.com*

INTRODUCTION

Oliver W. Harrington was a tremendously talented cartoonist whose work was never seen by most of America. For the largest part of his cartooning career, the work of "Ol Harrington" (as he originally signed his cartoons) appeared solely in newspapers aimed specifically at the African American community. That targeted audience allowed his work to comment on the racial issues afflicting America far more bluntly than any mainstream white paper would permit, while at the same time giving him the freedom to do broad humor presenting lively foibles of imperfect Black human beings without them being seen as symbolizing the race as a whole.

When it comes to the imperfection of human beings, Harrington's character Bootsie seems to have collected the whole set. This scheming, scamming, troublemaking womanizer first appeared in a December, 1935 installment of "Dark Laughter", Harrington's single-panel cartoon feature. The series had already been running for seven months before he appeared, but he ended up becoming the star. While the series would have a few other named characters and frequently just focused on unnamed members of New York's Black community, by far the greatest number of panels went to Bootsie L. Jackson. However, none of the dialogue was his. Whether Bootsie was on-panel or off, the caption would have someone else either talking to or about Bootsie. It was from that dialogue that we learned about his actions and the predicaments he found himself in; at times we would also learn that he was loved by the community as a whole, even when he wasn't liked by individuals.

Some of the situations he ended up in were a just result of his own actions, but others were not. Bootsie would endure indignities arising from the color of his skin, as well as from the sheer happenstance of being in the wrong place at the wrong time. The community may have had a default acceptance of this awkward soul, but the fates did not.

Over the years, "Dark Laughter" had switched from being exclusively in the New York-based *Amsterdam News* to being syndicated to a variety of Black papers. By the time of the panels in this volume, however, it was appearing exclusively in the *Pittsburgh Courier*, which was, despite its name, a national weekly which came out in a number of local editions. The body of this book includes all of the cartoons from July 31st, 1954 through the first strip of 1958, with two exceptions. The June 4th, 1955 strip included

June 4th, 1955

(misquoted) lyrics from the song "Our Love is Here to Stay" which presented licensing issues. The July 23rd strip from that same year has a different problem: we no longer know what the proper caption was. The one that it showed up with in the *Courier* was clearly not intended for the panel; the same caption appeared on the following week's cartoon, where it made a lot more sense.

During the period covered here, the feature went through two substantial shifts. On October 29, 1955, "Dark Laughter" moved from just being a typically-placed panel in the newspaper to being the cover feature on the Courier's new magazine section, giving Harrington even more room to unleash his rich and detailed art. That cover position would only last for a few months. When the cartoon moved inside the

July 23rd, 1955

magazine section, it was bestowed with a new title: "Bootsie". Even though Bootsie himself was not appearing in the cartoon as often as he had a decade before, he was still its most frequent star, and people had long since taken to calling the series itself by his name, so it seemed an obvious move to reflect that in the title.

In these cartoons, Harrington feels free to engage in the very real politics facing America, particularly those involving Black America, but is not afraid to have a bit of fun with it. He's willing to use the NAACP as the basis for some jokes, even though he himself had handled public relations for them in the 1940s.

Harrington had left the United States to live in Paris in 1951, where he drew all the cartoons in this collection. He was growing concerned not just about the situation of the United States in general but the specific interest that the U.S. government was taking in him and the statements he made in his work. He received asylum in then-Communist East Germany in 1961, and lived in Berlin from then until his death in 1995.

For those who did not live through the 1950s, notes in the back of this book explain many of the references to people and events of the time. If you have a larger interest in Harrington and his work, there are two other books currently in print collecting his cartoons. *Bootsie's War Years*, published (as is this volume) by About Comics, collects a run of "Dark Laughter" from 1941 through 1946. *Dark Laughter: The Satiric Art of Oliver W. Harrington*, edited by the late M. Thomas Inge and published by the University Press of Mississippi, collects cartoons from after the ones in this book, including ones he did for the New York-based Communist paper *The Daily Worker*.

"There's that Bootsie feller clownin' again. Shame he ain't got a little more hair on his head an' money in the bank... he would sure give Rubirosa a fit!"

"It's somethin' the old fool calls a Geiger Counter...
Brings it in here every time he orders fish!"

"Papa... you an' all them nice policemens can come on out now. I found 'im. He was hidin' in a sandpile!"

"Awright... come on and slide, Willy. There ain't goin' to be no blockin' this base 'case the Ladies Auxiliary Ebenezer, Eastern Conference, is got him well covered!"

"But, I don't mind so much havin' the man stick me with a bad fish-tail Cadillac. What worries me is what will the public think when they hears that Aaron, the figures king, was seen comin' into town ON FOOT!"

"Goodness, gracious, Baby Doll, how did I know it would be like this? I just told the real estate man to rent us a place for the Labor Day week-end where we wouldn't have to worry about no race problems!"

"It don't make no difference to me wha kind of school the NAACP says we got to go to... but I'm worried about old Rex here. He just naturally don't get along with white children's dogs!"

"Of course, Bootsie, of course, I would like to win the MISS SEPIA WORLD SERIES OF 1954 contest, but how do I know that YOU can guarantee it?"

"You can see for yourself that my boy here is honest. When he promises to fold in the tenth round, man, he REALLY folds!"

"Reverend, you must be out'a your natural mind, callin' me away from the TV when our own boys is battlin' for all of us in them world's series!"

"...and now we present a dynamic, young cullud leader who begged for this opportunity to explain why the good cullud folks of our fair state want us to KEEP our schools segregated and free!"

"All right now, everybody... three long rolls and a boom for
good old 'Destroyer' Johnston. One... two... three... !"

16

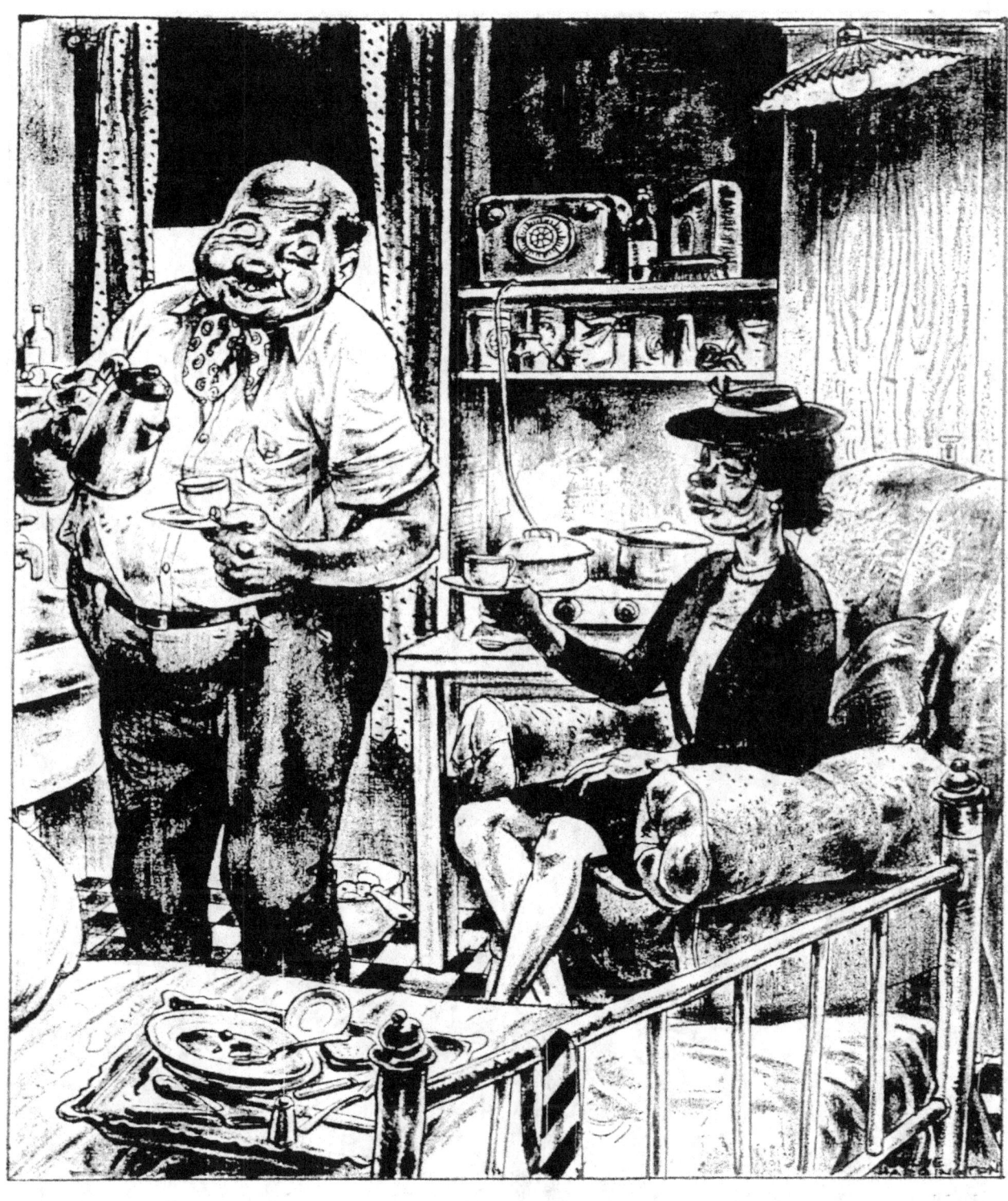

"Aw Brother Bootsie. NOW I understand why that there Marilyn Monroe put old Joe DiMaggio down. She must'a heard about your home cookin'."

"...and just like I said, everything was all quiet and dignified then this feller, Mister Bootsie, comes in an' starts a little discussion about who is the greatest, Doctor Bunche or Willie Mays."

"It's real nice to see Brother Bootsie's smilin' face amongst us again... BUT... sisters, remember that old Satan's got all kinds of smooth ways to really mess up a congregation!"

"Let's get away from here Bootsie. I don't like the looks of those kids. They're gettin' to be as dangerous as white childrens ever since they put 'em all together in one school!"

"Henry-Lee, sir! How many times have I told you that it ain't nice to throw rocks at folks' heads in the home?"

"Now Mama, please wait. I'm sick of listenin' to him blowin' his stack, too, but let's be practical and let's don't throw him out 'til AFTER Christmas!"

"Baby Doll, you know one thing? That NAACP has solid turned this town upside down. Why, only six months ago, who would'a guess that the department store would hire your Daddy-O for THIS job?"

"The card on it says 'Merry Christmas from Mister Bootsie' but knowin' him like we all do, I'm a'scared to open it!"

"Hi, Mabel... 'member them New Year's resolutions you an' me made? Well, I'm fixin' to take care of mine now... How you comin' with yours?"

"Don't be silly Mr. Bootsie, of course I'd like to be 'Miss Rheingold of 1955,' but how do I know that YOU can guarantee it?"

"Sure it's great, but it ain't practical. S'posin a cat gits real low on his loot... he sure can't set up housekeepin' in a chariot as little as that there!"

"An he's real hep, too, Bootsie. Man, you should'a been here the other day when he near 'bout bit off the landlord's arm!"

"Some ignorant folks say all this bad weather is from H-bomb an' some say it's the Russians. But that's all superstitious. Personally, 'tween me an' you, brother Bootsie, I think it's them SOUTHERN DEMOCRATS!"

"All right, Daddy-O, make up your mind before we goes over and asks Cleveland if they needs some flashy new material!"

"These, old man, are my ancestors. And by the way, since we're integrating you colored chaps down at the prep school, it would be a good idea if you'd begin assembling your own ancestral portraits!"

"Bootsie, remember how hard our folks had to fight before these eateries would LET US IN? Well, dig this bill... and then tell me who's goin' to fight to GET US OUT!"

"Now wait just one minute. What if he did squeeze all the shavin' cream into your new spring pearl grey... this ain't no way to teach him to do better."

"Sis Dawkins, come quick to the window. Cain't tell yet
though, whether it's goin' to be a funeral or weddin'!"

"Well, when Jackie was the onliest one we had on them ball teams it was real easy to root against the forces of evil. But the way it is now, a pore soul can't hardly root against nobody... it's terrible!"

"Well... I figgers it's more fun to watch them National League games 'cause it makes no diff'rence who wins 'cept when the Phillies are playin'..."

"Well, I was serving the reg'lar club members seven-up and stuff, and everything was real quiet and respectful. Then I head guest member, Brother Bootsie, and reg'lar member Weepin' Willie arguin' about could the good angel, Gabriel, fly faster than one of them new jets!"

"If Luther, that no-hitting boy friend of mine, don't raise his battin' average up to .300 this season, I'm gonna put him down. After all, a girl's gotta think about her future!"

"...and this one in 12-B is named Brother Bootsie. Pretend not to notice nothin'. He always puts on this act when he figures somebody's done something to him!"

...and so Bootsie asked me to give him a break and let him wax my car. Now he's been workin' on it six days, comes into the house for his regular meals, smokes my cigars, grabs my easy chair for the television programs. And now he just told me to bring in a bottle of scotch this evening because he's beginning to feel run down!"

"So you find a policeman and start hollerin' and cryin' like you're lost and don't know where you live at. They take you to the police station and feed you all the ice cream you can eat. They're real squares for lost kids!"

"All of them unschooled chicks can palpitate for Marlon Brando if they wants to, but this kind of carryin' on makes me know that Brother Bootsie L. Jackson is the onliest wild one for me!"

"Man, it hurst me to see old Ace actin' like that. Ever since they put him on the Express over at the Carlton Towers he won't speak to nobody, except maybe Lawyer Carter!"

"Sssssssh... Brother Bootsie. The feller is here to collect the installment on your clothes. I told him you was out of town but he said tha's all right, he'll set in front of your room an' wait 'till you comes back to town!"

"Pa, it hardly seems like it was only twenty years ago when he was the cutest little old thing on the avenue... An' we didn't have to friz up his hair like that neither!"

NOTE: ACTUAL DATE
550716

45

"Ought to be 'shamed of yourself, you dirty dog. All the rest of us is marchin'
forwards every day... en' JUST LOOK AT YOU!"

"Near about everybody onthe avenue think it's a dirty shame the way Brother Bootsie done you last evenin'. But what's wrong with that cat... don't he know the weather is too hot for that kind of stuff?"

"Oh, he's gentle as a woodland dove. Onliest time he ever really mangled
somebody was when the poor feller who used to have this room didn't
come up with last month's room rent!"

"The law just said we got to move it 'cause we been pared in the same spot for two weeks. But I cain't figure where we can raise enough for two gallons of gas!"

"Well, to tell the truth, Mom, I don't know what its 'sposed to be myself, but that's what the Government learned me on the G.I. Bill... and not only that, but the white folks buys 'em as fast as I can get the paint dry on 'em!"

"...So every time another feller just looks at me, Brother Bootsie starts actin' like Joe Louis. An' what gets me is that I ain't even goin' steady with him!"

"Sisters, I got a hand it to you. It's the greatest Labor Day outin' in the history of Shiloh Baptist... an' not even a bruise in the whole flock. But, the great mystery to me is how did you manage to keep that Brother Bootsie so full of peace an' contentment?"

"Madame, you just tell us who you want him to look like... Gregory Peck, Doctor Bunche, Anthony Eden... Just name it... and leave the rest to Ben's super-credit tailors!"

"...And gentlemen, ah don't care what that soopreme court says about it but ah ain't goin' to allow them two fair pearls of our great civilization to sit in the same schoolhouse with no savages!"

"It's nothing serious Sis Dawkins. Brother Bootsie's had a tough season pullin for Newcombe, Willie Mayes, Jackie, Doby, Minoso, Ernie Banks, Elston Howard, Sam Jones and the others. It stands to reason that ALL of 'em can't win the pennant!"

"Then the restaurant manager called the police and they made me eat in the cellar where they said it wuz real special. That's when I began to realize that they thought I was an Indian ambassador or sump'n!"

"Hello, is this The Courier? Well, you better send somebody right up here an' let 'im bring a photographer... I'm about to make your front page!"

"Well, we appreciates all that fire an' brimstone that them archangels is goin' to unload on 'em but look here Reverend what are WE goin' to do about Mississippi?"

"The folks I work for said I had to git psycho-analyzed, so I come here to this fool an' soon's I gits here he starts askin' me some real personal questions, you know, like playin' the dozens!"

"JACKSON, JACKSON, turn around. You're running the wrong way. You're running NORTH. The Alabama goal posts are south!"

"Brother Bootsie, remember last night how you was talkin' about buyin' me loads of furs and jewelry and Cadillacs? Well, how 'bout makin' it easy on yourself... and just buy me a beer?"

"The other roomers wouldn't complain so much 'bout you sawin' on that thing perfesser, if you would play somethin' nice sometimes... somethin' like 'WE'RE GONNA ROCK AROUN' THE CLOCK TONIGHT!'"

"I'm durn sure gonna contact the NAACP if we get out'a this, Bootsie. I know some of those folks down south has engineered this whole thing!"

"He's an exchange professor from some college in Mississippi, sent over to teach us underprivileged people freedom and democracy. But I wonder what he's carrying in that briefcase... a tommy-gun or a rope."

"Hey, look, y'all. Poor Brother Bootsie's over there cryin' over some beautiful chick who quit him when he lost his fortune in the '29 stock market crash. Now we all know it's a big fat lie, but come on, somebody, put a coin in the jukebox an' help him get his spirits back up!"

"Mr. Tiger Johnston, you better get up from there. We got our Christmas money ridin' on you and if you blow it... Brother, you're really gonna hurt!"

"Wait, fellers, hold it, for Pete's sake. They make me wear this outfit on my job down at the department store. Honest... I ain't the REAL one!"

"Well, awright, Daddy-o, you feelin' so roosterish this mornin', hep ME. What the –– IS so happy about it?"

"Aw right, Brother Bootsie, sir. Everyone here's a witness that I won the raffle. Now if you don't come up with a bird you're gonna look real silly layin' up in my oven all stuffed and swimmin' in gravy and sweet 'taters!"

"He kept tellin' me that our house wasn't big enough for both him and Spot.
Said one of 'em had to go.
I guess the fool didn't realize that I really LOVES this dog."

"Aw, stop bellyachin', mister. Ain't you got better sense that to get in the way of a flight of space ships?"

"Go 'head, Gaither, unloosen him. If he wounds 'm too deep,
we'll swear that the leash broke."

"Now, hold it, cuz. You know I'm willin' to do anything to help the race advance, but tell me one thing... do Doctor Bunche do foolishness like this?"

"Home of the brave... land of the free"

"But, baby doll, that's what's wrong with the whole world these days... folks just won't act friendly no more!"

"But Mister Mayor, sir, how can I keep my cullud brethren pacified if you Mister Policemans even whips ME at every meetin'?"

76

"I'm glad the folks called off that strike on the 28th. After all, what would the poor chicks do if WE went out on strike?"

"Hello. Is that you, Sis Dawkins? Well, I bet you can't guess what your little old girl friend has just went and did!"

"Now, ain't that the cutest thing you ever seen, bless their hearts? Jest look at how Brother Bootsie an' old Spot play together."

"Now you got to admit this ain't nice. An' just because I didn't join it, that notice was tacked up for all the roomers to join the NAACP before the first of the month."

"Goodness gracious, ain't that Brother Bootsie passin' by? You know, I think they plays a little too rough up there in his room!"

"Can me an' li'l brud here join up, ma'am? I realize he looks kinda small, but when he gits worked up he's a natural man-eatin' tiger!"

"...body all achin' an' wracked with pain..."

"Okay, Rasputin, here's your chance to make baseball history. We can't strike him out, so you see if you can't hypnotize 'im!"

"But, Honey, how will I ever get to be a real good driver if you're gonna look all mean an' evil every time I make a little mistake?"

"But Beauregard, Honey, did you explain to them that back home in Alabama
we treat our cullud servants just as if they were people?"

"An' Horse, I ain't been to that English class in near 'bout two months, but I be goin' there today to hep myself when it close down fer the vacation."

He says he's from some tribe called the Hockway-Gibblets, so whut kin we do...
give 'im a blood test?"

"She's great, Daddy, great! Never studied a note of music in her life!"

"Awright, Newk. Now just streak this one across his knees with some froo froo
on it. An' remember, Baby Doll, we're right behind you a hundred per cent!"

"There's a flock of foreign darkies in the gallery today to observe democracy in action, Senator Eastwater, so the chairman wanted me to ask you not to make your usual speech about what we ought'a do to keep OUR OWN darkies in their place!"

The way they been fightin' to keep these beaches jim-cro, I thought they must been swimmin' in champagne... but it ain't nothin but plain ocean!"

"Boys... we gotta face it... times have changed. They won't let us lynch 'em no more unless we can prove they're subversive!"

"Brother Bootsie, the way you put your heart an' soul in the 'Cha-Cha-Cha' I don't see why somebody don't run YOU for the vice president!"

"But, remember. Old Buddy, it was you who told the Senorita you was the only cullud bullfighter. An' after all, no matter how it turns out YOU WILL BE THE FIRST!"

"Well, no, Bootsie, I ain't sayin' you're really lyin', but how did you JUST find out you was really a Egyptian?"

"...and Reverend, you won't hardly believe it, but we been together for 25 years and there ain't never been one cross word between us."

"Goodness, gracious, Gaither... You reckon these fools expect us to run through this hassle every day an' do our HOMEWORK, TOO?"

"General Blotchit, you take your tanks and feint at Lynchville. General Pannick, you move into the county seat. And then in the confusion, my infantry will try to take little Luther to school!"

"Well, buddy, you can let 'em save YOU if you want to, but for me they would first have to scrape off that name!"

"An he been snappin' and snarlin' at folks ever since he started backbitin' that old root man over on the avenue!"

"Brothers! Sisters! If we're gonna treat our new candidate like this, what do you think them voters out there are gonna do to 'im?"

"Mister campaign manager, sir, Brother Coleman here, of our speakers' bureau, would like to kind'a suggest that headquarters get some CULLUD WRITERS to WRITE THEM SPEECHES FROM NOW ON!"

"Yes, Ma'm, they whupped us somethin awful, but, Mama, I swear...
these cats were usin' professionals!"

"Tain't none of my business if you ain't got nothin' to be thankful for, Brother Bootsie. After all, what do you want me to do about it?"

"Okay, John Foster Dulles, an' you too, Mister Kruschef. I know y'all would rather spend your time unsnarlin' the international situation. But I'm payin' you to clean up my back yard!"

"That's right, Brother Bootsie. Hit it one more lick... and win yourself a trip to where it's REAL warm!"

"Aw don't worry 'bout losing your money yet, Bootsie. Look at it this way man...
the kid is just showin' the fans his blindin' speed!"

"Body all achin' and wracked with pain... tote that barge, lift that bale..."

"Goodness gracious, Oswald, look, a colored Santa Claus!
What will that awful Supreme Court think up next?"

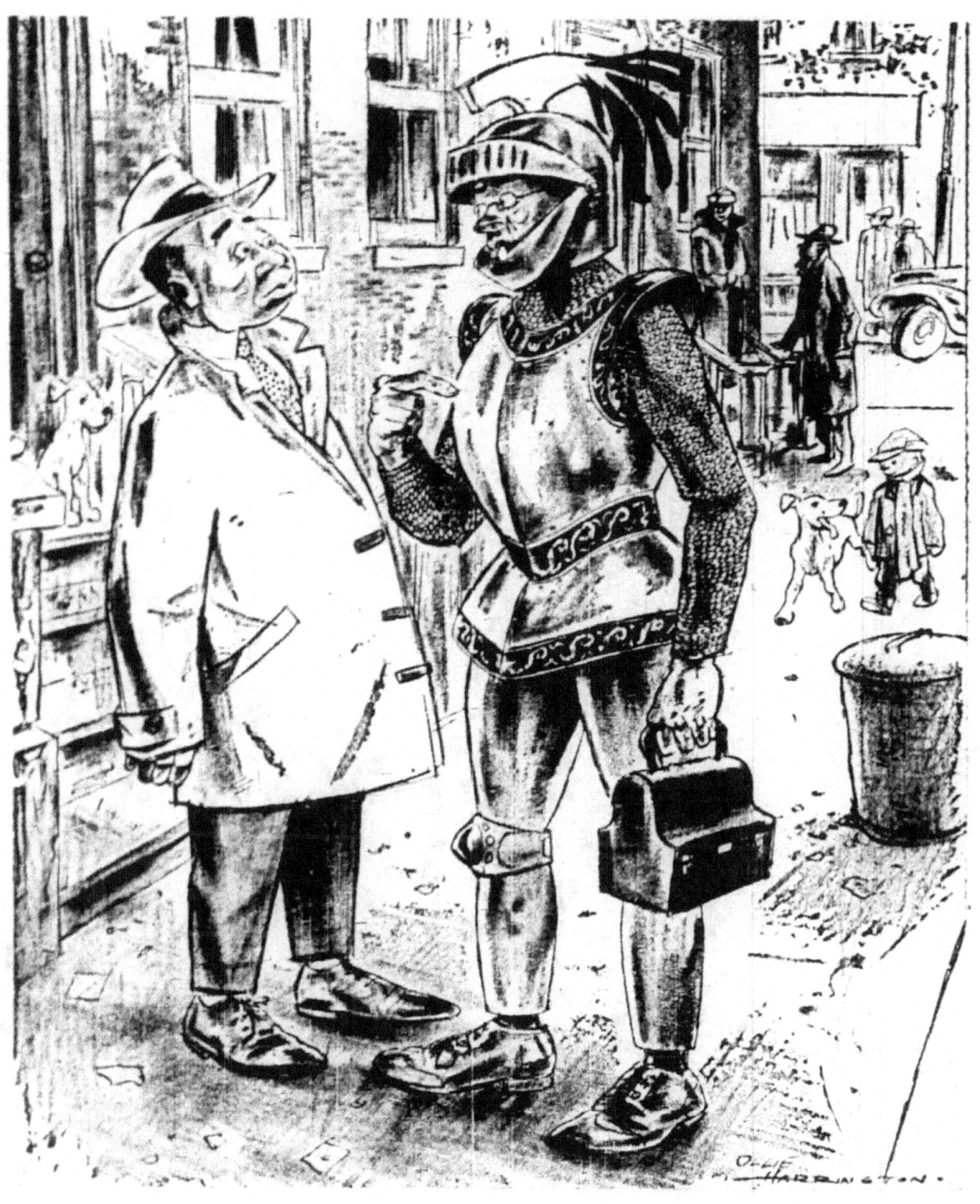

"Costume ball my foot! ...Man, I just bought a house in a all-white neighborhood an' this is the only way I can get home safe!"

"Honey, I guess our boy is smart as those professors say he is... but, sometimes, don't you get the feelin' that his brains is goin' to his head?"

"Senator Eastwater will lead our civil rights filibuster without the usual readin' of joke books, the Holy Bible, Aunt Mamie's cook books, and sech lichicher. You see, Suh, the Senator cain't read!"

"Eisenhower's done ruint me with all that integration stuff, Bootsie. Our folks is commencin' to act like they ain't got no more bad luck problems an' don't need old Nathan no more!"

"Madame Elsie, why don't you keep that hound chained up inside? One of these days he's gonna chew on somebody real important!"

"You guys hear the news? They're gonna let colored kids come to our school.
Now I bet'cha we have a REAL ball team this spring!"

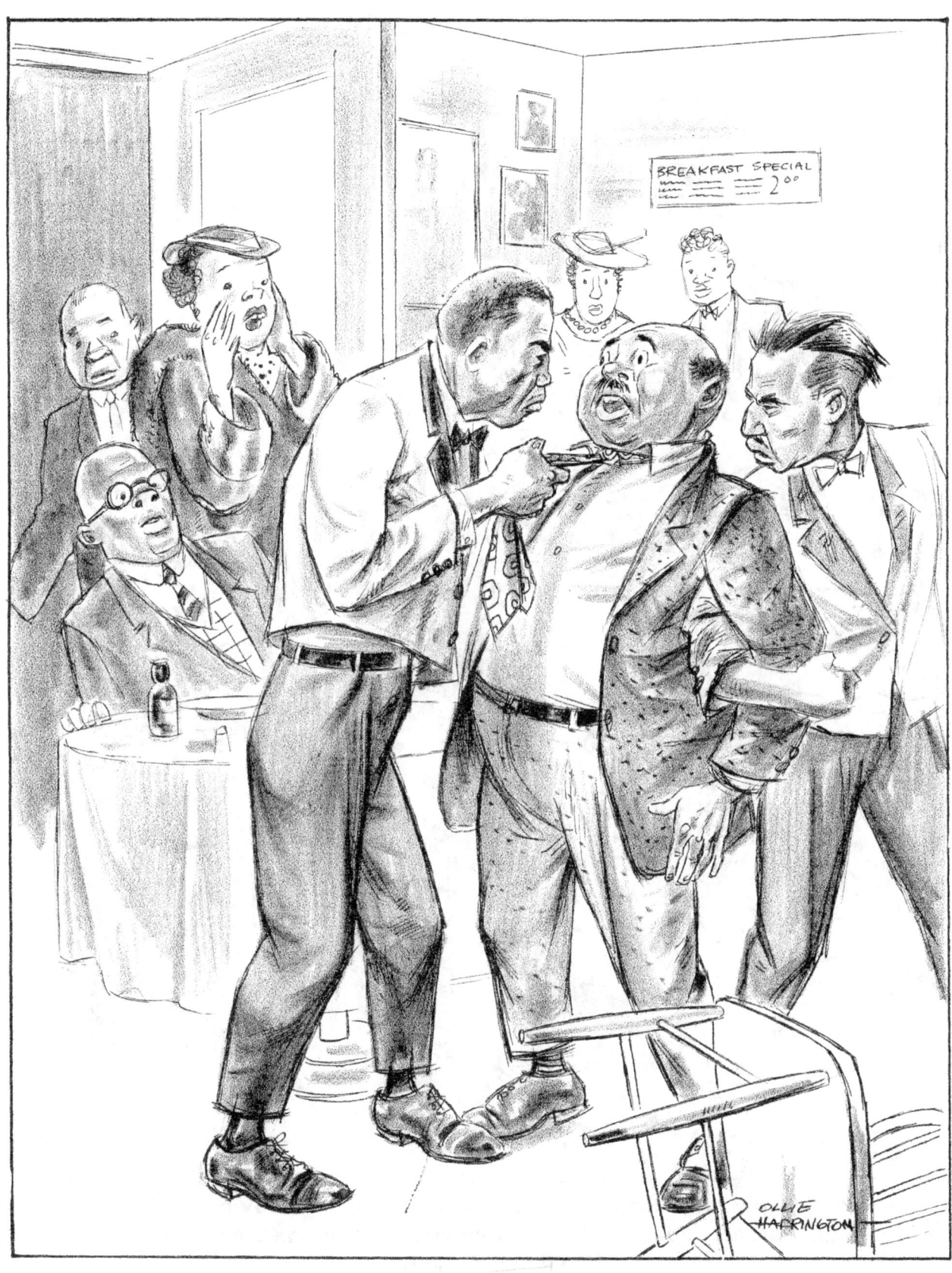

"Okay, Daddy, what kind'a discrimination you think you're pullin'? How come you always forget to bring your wallet when you come to a eat in a cullud joint?"

"An' we strongly recommend this outfit to our clients who buy property in white residential areas. You can deduct it from your income tax under medical and health expenditures!"

"Why you got to treat this pitchers like this so early in the season, Cuz? Man, we'll never get 'em interested in integration that way."

"...then this fool, Bootsie, hollers, 'Give everybody in the joint a drink on old Bootsie,' an' after I served 'em all, he commenced to gigglin' and says 'April Fool!'"

"Stop worryin', Honey, he'll be okay in there. After all, if we let him run wild in the street he's liable to wind up in somebody's jail an' ketch all kinds of complexes!"

"Goodness, gracious, 'Stretch,' las' time I saw you, you was more'n six feet tall.
What happened, Honey, somebody bad-mouth you?"

"Hey, Bootsie, Sis Dawkins just put a great big padlock on your door. Man, you're gonna look real crazy in that outfit you got on now!"

"Just look at 'em, Sister Abernathy. That's why when the white folks drive through here they thinks we don't love one another."

"...An I'm tired listin' to you ringside cats loud mouthin' about how I'm lettin' the race down. So, okay, Daddy-o, you an' the race take it from here!"

"Say, professor, some character name of Ike is callin' from Washington, wantin' to know if you and Brother Bootsie's got his global strategy figgered out yet...!"

"Rev', Old Boy, last evenin' I tried that stuff you're always stressin' about turnin' the other cheek... and now I'm kinda wanderin' if you practices what you preach?"

"Oh, poor Shorty. But I told him a million times not to mess with Spot when I ain't here. Man, that hound is tempermental!"

"Explain to the... fools that back home we're paid up supporters
of the NAACP."

"...Down at the bank they gave Herbert his 25-year faithful service medal. Now the children has to salute 'im before they goes up to bed!"

"...An' I don't see why you got to laugh at Old Bootsie. After all, he's jus'
showin' the public that he's a sportin' type!"

"Quick, baby, run in and telephone the NAACP that a cat who's three-quarters Cherokee is about to mess with a Afro-American! What can they do real quick?"

"See there? If folks like you had'a paid up their NAACP dues, our folks wouldn't get treated like this!"

"...and don't you dare seat any of those horrid Negroes near us tonight. The last time you did I suffered from indigestion for two full days!"

"No, poor old Henry won't be down this year. He passed on last February.
That's why I'm wearin' all this durned mournin'."

"...So me and ol' Spot was swimmin' underwater an' came right up under
Brother Bootsie, you know, kind'a like we was sharks..."

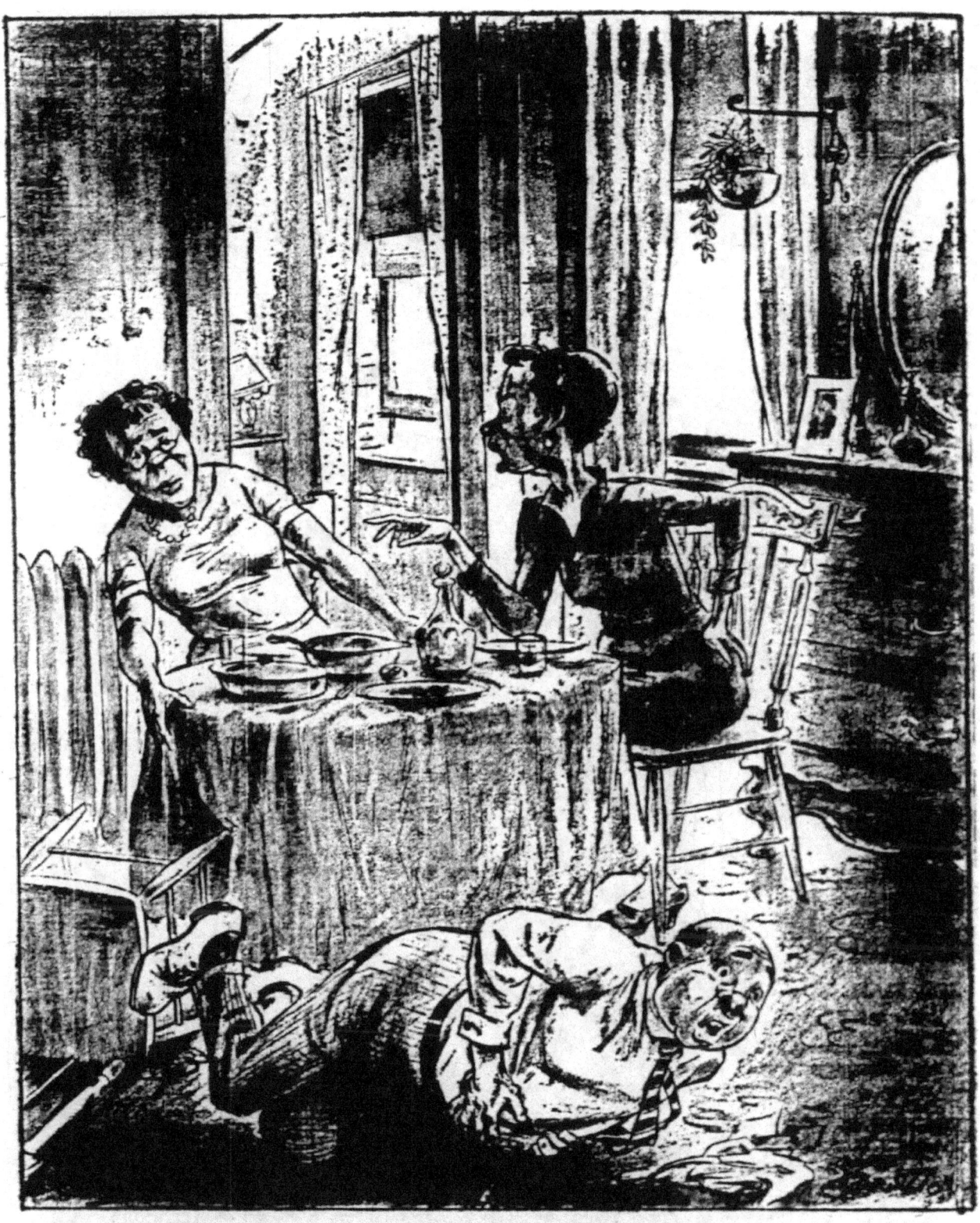

"Somebody ought'a make those butchers stop sellin' all their bad meat to us cullud folks. Now just suppose that had'a been that nice preacher we invited up for a little light lunch?"

"'Scuse me, Doctor, Sir, but don't you think we settin' a little low in the water?"

"At first we thought the Russians had went an' dropped one on us. You can imagine how relieved we were when we found out it was only the White Citizens Council bombin' our house agin'!"

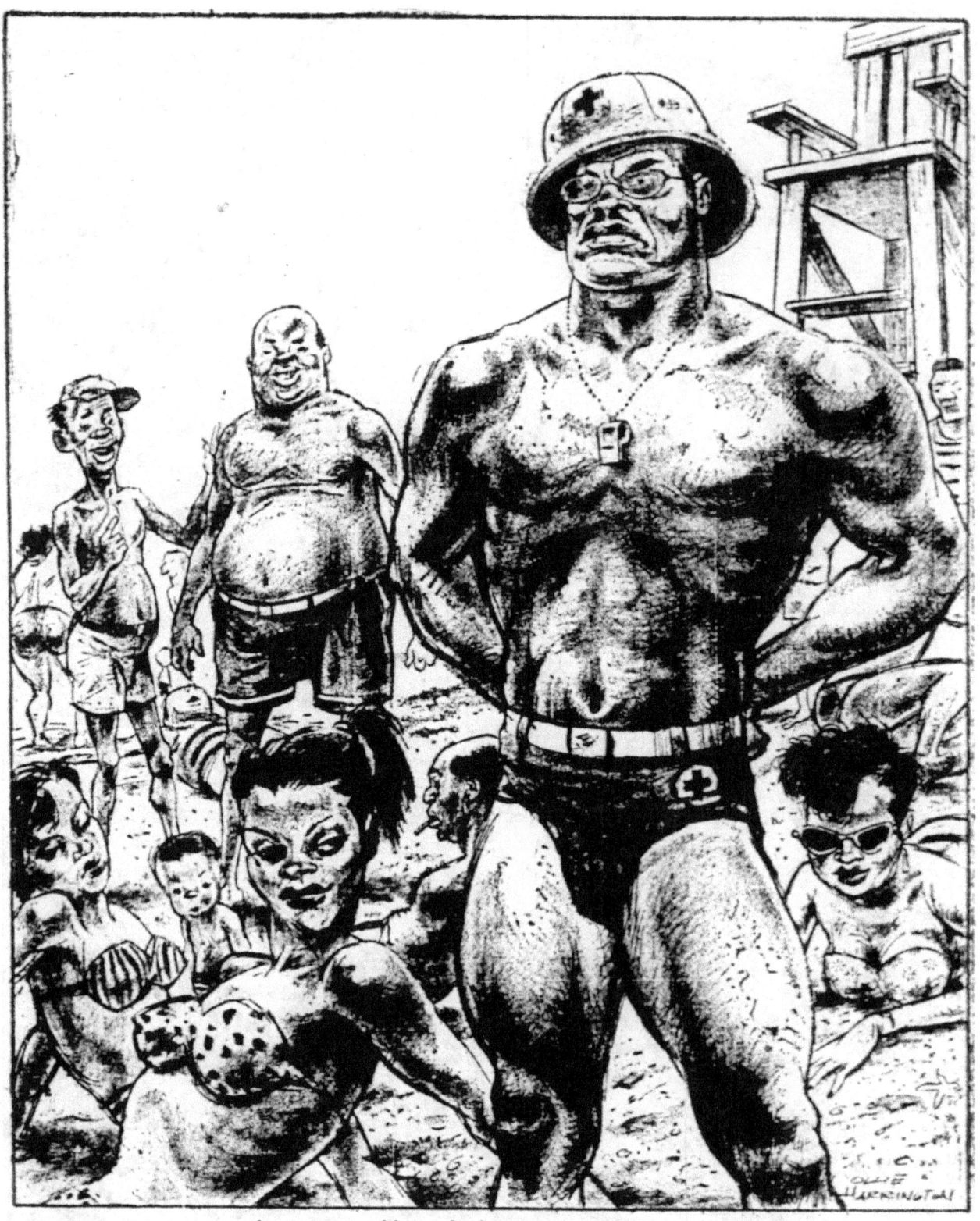

"Bootsie, I swear he's cryin' like a baby. Next week he's got to put on some clothes an' compete with us personality cats."

"...And havin' courageously held your position in the face of a suicidal charge
by several frenzied Niggra children trying to enter the General Lee Elementary
School, our great Governor bestows Dixie's noblest medal for gallantry in action!"

"No, I ain't scared; but you gotta admit this is one heck of a way to get an education!"

"Patrons is all complainin' because you cats ain't showin' your gums and actin' like happy children of nature... so everybody stays after work tonight and we're gonna rehearse!"

"It's about time for that durn Bootsie to start hammerin' on the walls 'bout my radio playin' too loud. But, tonight, I'm gonna give that fool some REAL hi-fi sound!"

"Hello, Doctor Harold Flemings? Well, I'd like you to come over 'cause Brother Bootsie got to rushin' around in my parlor... an' I kind'a think he strained himself!"

"Doctor Jenkins, before you read us your paper on inter-stellar gravitational tensions in thermo-nuclear propulsion, would you sing a grand old spiritual?"

"You the loud-mouthed gentleman been out here hollerin' for sump'n sharp enough to cut into that Jersey Tom Special?"

"Harris, the entire nation is watching to see how these Southern boys react to you. If there's any foul play we'll be on the phone to the White House before you even get to the hospital!"

"An' girl, las' year I made the mistake of lettin' him run loose before he had bought me even the first present... an' the rascal went an' cut out two weeks before Christmas!"

"If they had let some of us cullud kids go to their schools maybe WE could'a helped 'em get one of them things off the ground."

"It's got three sticks of dynamite in it, an' exactly at 12 midnight, when
Bootsie an' them other fools commence hollering 'Happy New Year'...
the whole... house blows up!"

Notes

5: The five-times married Porfirio Rubirosa was a Dominican sportsman, diplomat, and celebrated playboy.

6: A Geiger counter detects radiation. In 1954, irradiated fish were a concern in the wake of the H-bomb tests on the Bikini atoll.

9: "Figures" would be the illegal lottery more commonly known as "numbers".

11: NAACP is the National Association for the Advancement of Colored People, a leading civil rights group since its founding in 1909.

12: The Miss Sepia beauty pageants were founded in 1931, in reaction to Black women being excluded from the existing pageants of the day.

14: In the 1954 Major League Baseball World Series, the Manhattan-based New York Giants defeated the Cleveland Indians.

17: Movie star Marilyn Monroe filed for divorce from New York Yankees centerfielder Joe DiMaggio in October 1954, after nine months of marriage.

18: Doctor Ralphe Bunche, a member of the American delegation at the United Nations, became the first person of African descent to win a Nobel Prize when he received the Nobel Peace Prize in 1950. Willie Mays, then playing center field for the New York Giants, was in the midst of a baseball career that would see him make the All-Star team in 20 different seasons.

26: "Miss Rheingold" was a popularity contest used to promote Rheingold Beer. Tens of millions of votes would be cast each year to select one woman from six finalists.

35: After Jackie Robinson broke Major League Baseball's "color line" by becoming the first baseman for the Brooklyn Dodgers in 1947, it was less than three months before other teams began to take on Black players.

36: The Philadelphia Phillies were the last all-white team in Major League Baseball, finally taking a Black player in 1957.

42: White actor Marlon Brando played the leader of a motorcycle gang in the 1953 film *The Wild One*.

43: Former NAACP lawyer Russell L. Carter had, by this point, been named a judge in Ohio.

50: The G.I. Bill — a nickname for The Servicemen's Readjustment Act of 1944 — provides US military veterans with funding for college and other training programs, among other benefits.

51: Joe Louis, an African-American boxer, was the world's heavyweight boxing champion continuously from 1937 to 1949.

53: American movie star Gregory Peck didn't star in any films that came out in 1955, the year of this cartoon. Doctor Ralph Bunche was then the chief mediator at the United Nations. Anthony Eden was then Prime Minister of the United Kingdom.

54: The U.S. Supreme Court had ruled against school segregation in the landmark 1954 case *Brown v. Board of Education*.

55: In 1955, Black ballplayers Don Newcombe and Jackie Robinson were both playing for the Brooklyn Dodgers, Willie Mays for the New York Giants, Larry Doby for the Cleveland Indians, Minnie Miñoso for the Chicago White Sox, Ernie Banks and Sam Jones for the Chicago Cubs, and Elston Howard for the New York Yankees.

56: In August, 1955, Gaganvihari Lallubhai Mehta, India's ambassador to the U.S., was moved from the main dining room of the Horizon House restaurant at the Houston, Texas, airport because the management thought he was Black. Texas law forbade serving white and Black customers in the same room.

58: Mississippi refused to desegregate their schools for more than a decade after the Supreme Court ruling in *Brown v. Board of Education* called for it.

59: "The Dozens" is a sporting battle of insults.

62: "Rock Around the Clock" was a big hit for Bill Haley & The Comets in 1954.

73: If you're reading straight through these notes, you already know that Ralph Bunche was the Black chief mediator for the United Nations who received the Nobel Peace Prize.

83: The singer is singing "Ol' Man River", a song sung by a Black longshoreman in the 1927 stage musical Show Boat.

90: "Newk" would be Black baseball player Don Newcombe, who had was credited with 27 wins out of the 34 games he pitched for the Brooklyn Dodgers in the 1956 season.

92: "Jim-cro" is a stylization of "Jim Crow," the common name for racial segregation laws of the time.

98–99: In some locales, school integration was fiercely opposed by local white residents, causing the need for government forces to protect children entering the school.

106: John Foster Dulles was the United States Secretary of State at the time. Nikita Khrushchev was serving as the First Secretary of the Communist Party of the Soviet Union.

109: As with a previous cartoon, the singer is singing "Ol' Man River" from the 1927 stage musical *Show Boat*.

139: White Citizens Councils were created throughout the American South with the goal of preventing school desegregation.

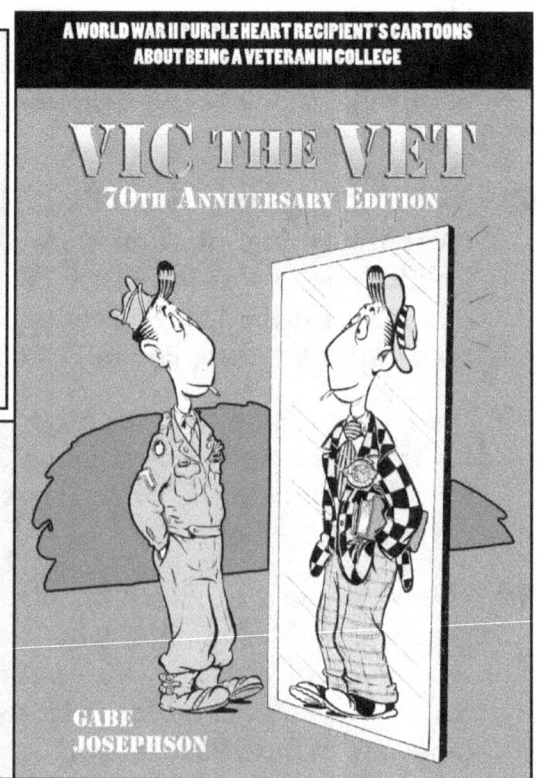

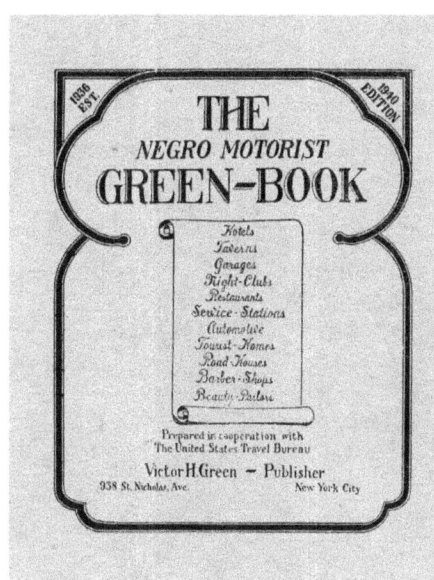

www.ingramcontent.com/pod-product-compliance
Lightning Source LLC
Chambersburg PA
CBHW081228020726
47503CB00011B/2944